Cow In The Garden

Larry Yarrow

Print information available on the last page

Rev. date: 08/30/2017

Illustrated by: Shannen Marie Paradero

To order additional copies of this book, contact:
Xlibris
1-888-795-4274
www.Xlibris.com
Orders@Xlibris.com

To my Mother, Deloris,

Kay, Terah and Shane,

Ellen Lucy Robertson,

and to all musicians everywhere.

Potatoes: Excellent source of vitamin C, Fiber, Iron and Potassium.

Corn: Protein, Fiber, Carbohydrates, Thiamine and Vitamin B6.

Tomatoes: Promotes heart health that helps bones stay strong . Good for digestion, skin and helps prevent cancer and strokes.

Cabbage: Good source of fiber, vitamins B6 and B5, manganese and thiamine.

Squash: Vitamin E and B6, Niacin, manganese and potassium.

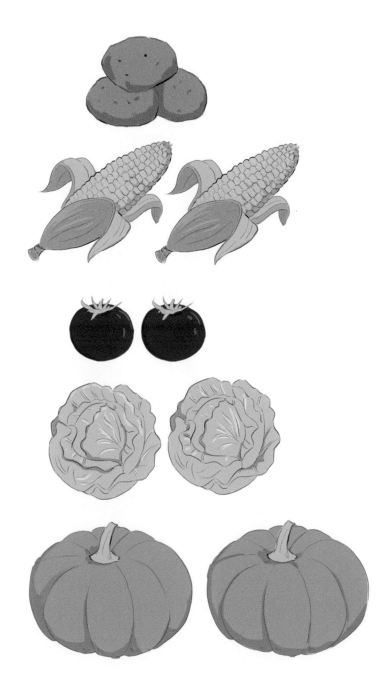

We were dancing in the living room listening to the radio

When I heard a sudden sound from out of our back yard

I flicked on the porch light said Kate I beg your pardon

Someone left the gate open our cow is in the garden

So stop the music cool the dance

That cow is stomping all over our plants

Get her out of there chase her away

Gonna send that old moo cow to bed without any hay

She stomped on our potatoes stomped on our corn

Smashed all our tomatoes sure as you're born

Damaged the cabbage squished all the squash

Delicious food we grew is nearly all lost

We finally got her rounded up and put back in the barn

I never knew a bovine that would cause a garden harm

I chewed her out she chewed her cud and didn't give a darn

Just shook my head went to bed and set the clocks' alarm

But all night long she kept mooing loud

I wondered how I could shut-up that old cow

If she don't stop mooing that old milk cow song

We'll never get any sleep at all

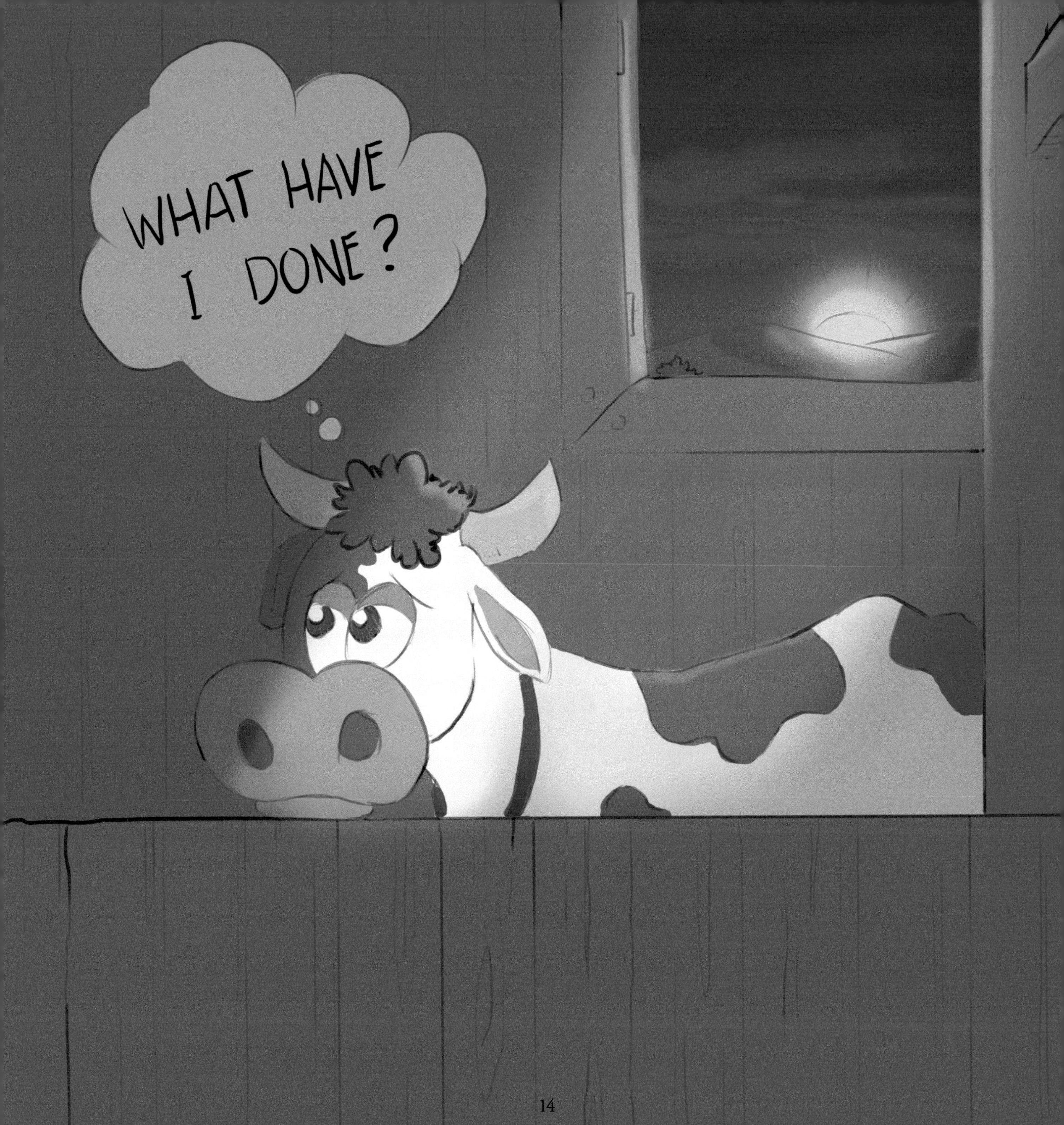
WHAT HAVE I DONE?

Then suddenly it got quiet with the approaching dawn

That cow was thinking about all the damage she had done

The wasted vitamins and ruined healthy nutrition

She now knows to appreciate the nourishment involved

So start up the music get up and dance

That cow is looking for a second chance

To show everybody what we really should eat

From infancy childhood to when we get big

Printed in the United States
by Baker & Taylor Publisher Services